DUE DATE

MAR 10 1992		
JUL 30 1992	APR 14 1994	
AR 29 1993	FEB 13 1995	
AUG 27 1993		
	MAR 22 1997	
NOV 13 1993	APR 16 1998	
APR 14 1994		
	AUG 12 1998	
SEP -1 1999	SEP -1 1999	
JUN -4 2001	JUN -4 2001	
AUG 19 2002	JUL 10 2001	
	JUL 17 2002	
	AUG 10 2002	

Printed
in USA

LULLABY
OF THE WIND

LULLABY
OF THE WIND

by Karen Whiteside

pictures by Kazue Mizumura

HARPER & ROW, PUBLISHERS

Library of Congress Cataloging in Publication Data
Whiteside, Karen.
  Lullaby of the wind.

  Summary: The wind sings lullabies to a candle, the
curtains, rain, trees, and the sea before finally
sending a child to sleep in her mama's arms.
  [1. Bedtime—Fiction.   2. Lullabies]   I. Title.
PZ8.3.W5885Lu 1984   [E]   83-47702
ISBN 0-06-026411-X
ISBN 0-06-026412-8 (lib. bdg.)

For Larry and Anika with love

It is nighttime.

Wind is singing lullabies.

Wind is telling everyone

to go to sleep.

In a child's bedroom,
wind sings a lullaby to a candle.
Candle's flame bows to the wind,
and then it falls asleep.

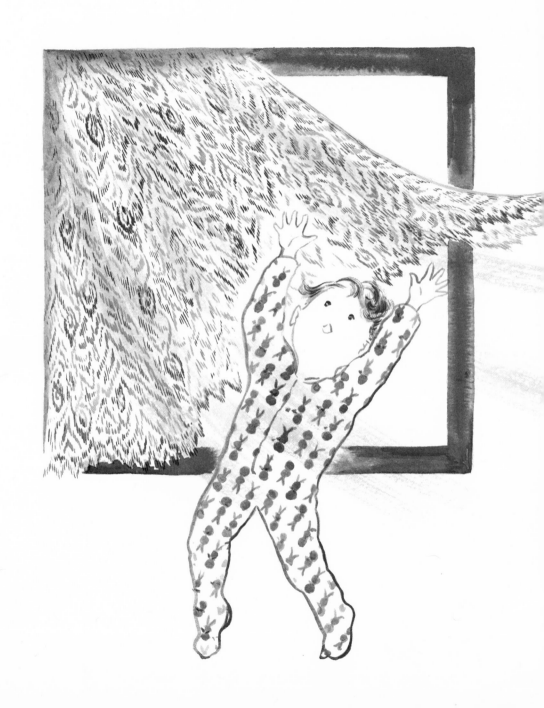

In the window,

wind sings a lullaby to the curtains.

Curtains swing,

wind holds them high

and they fall asleep in the arms of wind.

Outside the window,
wind sings a lullaby
to the drizzling rain.
Raindrops fall asleep;
in a dream
they drip down the window.

Down the street,

wind sings a lullaby to the trees.

Trees dance to wind's song;

leaves dance and then they fall asleep.

In the alley,

wind sings a lullaby to a cat.

Cat curls up and closes his eyes;

he falls asleep to the song of wind.

Down by the river,
wind sings a lullaby to a sea gull.
Sea gull falls asleep;
in his sleep
he rides on wind's wings.

Way across the land,
wind sings a lullaby to the sea.
Sea falls asleep;
waves of the sea roll over
in their sleep.

Up in the sky,

wind sings a lullaby to the clouds.

Clouds fall asleep;

they float through the purple sky

in a dream.

Back in the bedroom,
wind sings a lullaby to the child.
The child closes her eyes
and falls asleep in her mama's arms.